HORRID
HENRY'S
REVENGE

Francesca Simon spent her childhood on the
beach in California, and then went to Yale
and Oxford Universities to study medieval
history and literature. She now lives in
London with her English husband and their
son. When she is not writing books she is
doing theatre and restaurant reviews or
chasing after her Tibetan Spaniel, Shanti

Also by Francesca Simon

HORRID HENRY'S
REVENGE

Francesca Simon
Illustrated by Tony Ross

Orion
Children's Books

First published in Great Britain in 2001
by Orion Children's Books
a division of the Orion Publishing Group Ltd
Orion House
5 Upper St Martin's Lane
London WC2H 9EA
An Hachette UK Company

Text © Francesca Simon 2001
Illustrations © Tony Ross 2001

The moral right of Francesca Simon and Tony Ross
to be identified as author and illustrator
of this work has been asserted.

The Orion Publishing Group's policy is to use papers that
are natural, renewable and recyclable products and
made from wood grown in sustainable forests. The logging
and manufacturing processes are expected to conform to
the environmental regulations of the country of origin.

A catalogue record for this book is available
from the British Library.

Printed in Great Britain by
Clays Ltd, St Ives plc

www.orionbooks.co.uk

For Chris Harris, Wendy Kinnard,
Ben, Sophie and Jessica with love

CONTENTS

1

HORRID HENRY'S REVENGE

SLAP!

"Waaaaaaaaaa!"

SLAP! SLAP! PINCH!

"Muuuummmmmm!" shrieked Peter. "Henry slapped me!"

"Did not!"

"Did too! And he pinched me!"

"Stop being horrid, Henry!" said Mum.

"But Peter started it!" shouted Henry.

"Did not!" wailed Peter. "Henry did!"

Horrid Henry glared at Perfect Peter.

Perfect Peter glared at Horrid Henry.

Mum went back to writing her letter. Horrid Henry lashed out and pulled Peter's hair. He was a coiling cobra unleashing his venom.

"Eowwwwww!" shrieked Peter.

"Go to your room, Henry!" screamed Dad. "I've had just about enough of you today!"

"Fine!" shouted Henry. "I hate you, Peter!" he shrieked, stomping up to his bedroom and slamming the door as loud as he could.

It was so unfair! Peter was never sent to his room. Horrid Henry was sent to *his* so often he might as well live there full-time. Henry couldn't burp without Peter trying to get him into trouble.

"Mum! Henry's dropping peas on the floor!"

"Dad! Henry's sneaking sweets!"

"Mum! Henry's eating on the new sofa!"

"Dad! Henry's playing on the phone!"

Horrid Henry had had enough. He was sick and tired of that goody-goody ugly toad tattle-tale brat.

But what could he do about Peter? He'd tried selling him as a slave to Moody Margaret, but Henry didn't think she'd buy him again. If only he knew how to cast spells, he could turn Peter into a toad or a beetle or a worm. Yes! Wouldn't that be great! He'd charge everyone 10p to look at his brother, the worm. And if Peter-worm *ever* wriggled out of line he'd be fish bait. Horrid Henry smiled.

11

Then he sighed. The truth was, he was stuck with Peter. But if he couldn't sell Peter, and he couldn't turn Peter into a worm, he *could* get Peter into trouble.

Unfortunately, getting Perfect Peter into trouble was easier said than done. Peter never did anything wrong. Also, for some reason he didn't always trust Henry. The only way to get Peter into trouble was to trick him. And if it took all year, Horrid Henry vowed he would come up with a perfect plan. A plan to get Peter into trouble. Big, big, BIG trouble. That would be almost as good as turning him into a worm.

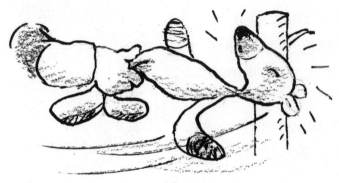

"I'll pay you back, Peter," growled Henry, thumping his teddy, Mr Kill, against the bedpost. "I will be revenged on you!"

"What are you doing, Henry?" asked Peter.

"Nothing," said Horrid Henry. Quickly he stopped poking around the old apple tree at the end of the garden and stood up.

"You're doing something, I know you are," said Peter.

"Whatever I'm doing is none of your business, telltale," said Henry.

"Have you found something?" said Peter. He looked at the base of the tree. "I don't see anything."

"Maybe," said Henry. "But I'm not telling you. You can't keep a secret."

"Yes I can," said Peter.

13

"And you're too young," said Henry.

"No I'm not," said Peter. "I'm a big boy. Mum said so."

"Well, too bad," said Horrid Henry. "Now go away and leave me alone. I'm doing something important."

Perfect Peter slunk off about ten paces, then turned and stood still, watching Henry.

Horrid Henry continued to prowl around the tree, staring intently at the grass. Then he whistled and dropped to his knees.

14

"What have you found?" said Perfect Peter eagerly. "Treasure?"

"Much better than treasure," said Horrid Henry. He picked something up and hid it in his hand.

"Oh show me," said Peter. "Please. Oh please!"

Horrid Henry considered.

"If – and I mean if – I tell you something, do you swear by the sacred oath of the purple hand to say nothing about this to anyone?"

"I swear," said Peter.

"Even if you're being tortured by aliens?"

"I WON'T TELL!" shrieked Peter.

Horrid Henry put his finger to his lips, then tiptoed away from the tree to his fort. Peter followed.

"I don't want them to know I'm telling you," he whispered, when they were hidden behind the branches. "Otherwise they'll disappear."

"Who?" whispered Peter.

"The fairies," said Henry.

"Fairies," squeaked Perfect Peter. "You mean you've seen—"

"Shh!" hissed Horrid Henry. "They'll run away if you tell anyone."

"I won't," said Perfect Peter. "Promise. Oh wow, fairies! In our garden! Oh, Henry! Fairies! Just wait till I tell my teacher."

"NO!" screamed Horrid Henry. "Tell no one. Especially grown-ups. Fairies hate grown-ups. Grown-ups stink to fairies."

Perfect Peter clasped his hand over his mouth.

"Sorry, Henry," he said.

Horrid Henry opened his hand. It was sprinkled with gold glitter.

"Fairy dust," said Horrid Henry.

"It looks just like glitter," said Perfect Peter.

"Of course it looks like glitter," said Horrid Henry. "Where do you think glitter comes from?"

"Wow," said Peter. "I never knew glitter came from fairies."

"Well now you know," said Henry.

"Can I see them, Henry?" asked Peter.

"Please let me see them!"

"They only come out to dance at dead of night," said Horrid Henry.

"Past my bedtime?" said Perfect Peter.

"'Course," said Horrid Henry. "Midnight is the fairy hour."

"Oh," said Peter. His face fell.

"Told you you were too young," said Henry.

"Wait," said Perfect Peter. "If they only come out at midnight, how come *you've* seen them?"

"Because I've sneaked out and hidden up the apple tree," said Horrid Henry. "It's the only way."

"Ah," said Perfect Peter. "Umm," said Perfect Peter. "Ooh," said Perfect Peter.

"I'm going to see them tonight," said Henry casually.

"Do you think you could ask them to come before seven thirty?" said Peter.

"Oh yeah, right," said Henry. "Hiya, fairies! My brother wants you to dance for him at seven o'clock." "Sure thing, Henry," said Henry in a high squeaky fairy voice. "You don't speak to fairies. You have to hide up the tree. If they knew I'd seen them they'd run away and never come back."

Perfect Peter was in torment. He wanted to see the fairies more than anything in the world. But getting out of bed after lights out! And sneaking outside! And climbing the tree! And on a school night! It was too much.

"I can't do it," whispered Perfect Peter.

Henry shrugged. "Fine, baby. You need your rest."

Peter hated being called baby. Next to "smelly nappy", it was the worst name Henry could call him.

"I am not a baby."

19

"Yes you are," said Henry. "Now go away, baby. Just don't blame me when you spend the rest of your life moaning that you missed seeing real live fairies."

Horrid Henry started to leave the fort.

Perfect Peter sat very still. Fairies! But was he brave enough, and bad enough, to sneak out of the house – at night?

"Don't do it," whispered his angel.

"Do it," squeaked his devil, a very small, sad, puny creature who spent his life inside Peter's head squashed flat by the angel.

20

"I'll come," said Perfect Peter.
YES! thought Horrid Henry.
"Okay," said Henry.

Tiptoe. Tiptoe. Tiptoe.
  Tiptoe. Tiptoe. Tiptoe.
  Horrid Henry sneaked down the stairs.
Perfect Peter followed him. Softly, Henry
opened the back door, and slipped
outside. He held a small torch.
  "It's so dark!" said Perfect Peter, staring
into the shadows at the bottom of the
garden.
  "Quiet," whispered Horrid Henry.
"Follow me."

They crept across the lawn down to the apple tree.

Perfect Peter looked up into the ghostly branches.

"It's too high for me to climb," he protested.

"No it isn't, I'll give you a leg up," said Horrid Henry. He grabbed Peter and shoved him up. Peter caught the lowest branch and started to climb.

"Higher," said Henry. "Go as high as you can."

Peter climbed. And climbed. And climbed.

"This is high enough," squeaked Perfect Peter. He settled himself on a branch, then cautiously looked down. "I don't see anything," he whispered.

There was no reply.

"Henry?" said Peter.

"Henry!" said Peter, a little louder.

Still there was no reply. Perfect Peter peered into the darkness. Where could he be? Could Henry have been kidnapped by fairies? Oh no!

Then Perfect Peter saw a dreadful sight.

There was his brother, darting back into the house!

Perfect Peter did not understand. Why wasn't Henry waiting to see the fairies? Why had he left Peter?

And then suddenly Peter realised the terrible truth. His treacherous brother had tricked him.

"I'll get you – you're gonna be in big trouble – I'll – I'll – " squeaked Peter. Then he stopped. His legs were too short to reach the lower branch.

Perfect Peter couldn't climb down. He was stuck up a tree, all alone, at night. He had three choices. He could wait and hope that Henry would come back and help him. Fat chance. Or he could sleep all night in the damp, cold, scary, spooky tree. Or he could—

"MUUUUUUUM!" screamed Peter.

"DAAAADD!"

Mum and Dad stumbled out into the darkness. They were furious.

"What are you doing out here, Peter!" screamed Mum.

"You horrible boy!" screamed Dad.

"It was Henry's fault!" shrieked Peter, as Dad helped him down. "He brought me here! He made me climb up."

"Henry is sound asleep in bed," said Mum. "We checked on the way out."

"I am so disappointed in you, Peter," said Dad. "No stamp collecting for a month."

"WAAAAAAAH!" wailed Peter.

"Shuddup!" screamed the neighbours. "We're trying to sleep."

Meanwhile, back in bed, Horrid Henry stretched and smiled. No one could pretend to be asleep better than Horrid Henry.

What a perfect revenge, he thought. Peter in trouble. Henry in the clear. He

was so excited he never noticed his torn,
dirty, leafy pyjamas.

Unfortunately, the next morning,
Mum did.

2

HORRID HENRY'S COMPUTER

"No, no, no, no, no!" said Dad.

"No, no, no, no, no!" said Mum.

"The new computer is only for work," said Dad. "My work, Mum's work, and school work."

"Not for playing silly games," said Mum.

"But everyone plays games on their computer," said Henry.

"Not in this house," said Dad. He looked at the computer and frowned. "Hmmn," he said. "How do you turn this thing off?"

"Like this," said Horrid Henry. He pushed the "off" button.

"Aha," said Dad.

It was so unfair! Rude Ralph had Intergalactic Robot Rebellion. Dizzy Dave had Snake Masters Revenge III. Moody Margaret had Zippy Zappers. Horrid Henry had Be a Spelling Champion, Virtual Classroom, and Whoopee for Numbers. Aside from Beefy Bert, who'd been given Counting Made Easy for Christmas, no one else had such awful software.

"What's the point of finally getting a computer if you can't play games?" said Horrid Henry.

"You can improve your spelling," said Perfect Peter. "And write essays. I've already written one for school tomorrow."

"I don't want to improve my

spelling!" screamed Henry. "I want to play games!"

"I don't," said Perfect Peter. "Unless it's "Name that Vegetable" of course."

"Quite right, Peter," said Mum.

"You're the meanest parents in the world and I hate you," shrieked Henry.

"You're the best parents in the world and I love you," said Perfect Peter.

Horrid Henry had had enough. He leapt on Peter, snarling. He was the Loch Ness monster gobbling up a thrashing duck.

"OWWWWWW!" squealed Peter.

"Go to your room, Henry!" shouted Dad. "You're banned from the computer for a week."

"We'll see about that," muttered Horrid Henry, slamming his bedroom door.

Snore. Snore. Snore.

Horrid Henry sneaked past Mum and Dad's room and slipped downstairs.

There was the new computer. Henry sat down in front of it and looked longingly at the blank screen.

How could he get some games? He had 53p saved up. Not even enough for Snake Masters Revenge I, he thought miserably. Everyone he knew had fun on their computers. Everyone except him. He loved zapping aliens. He loved marshalling armies. He loved ruling the world. But no. His yucky parents would only let him have educational games. Ugh. When he was king anyone who wrote an educational game would be fed to the lions.

Horrid Henry sighed and switched on the computer. Maybe some games were hidden on the hard disk, he thought hopefully. Mum and Dad were scared of computers and wouldn't know how to look.

The word "Password" flashed up on the screen.

I know a good password, thought Horrid Henry. Quickly he typed in "Smelly Socks".

SMELLY SOCKS

Then Horrid Henry searched. And searched. And searched. But there were no hidden games. Just boring stuff like Mum's spreadsheets and Dad's reports.

Rats, thought Henry. He leaned back in the chair. Would it be fun to switch around some numbers in Mum's dreary spreadsheet? Or add a few words like "yuck" and "yah, boo, you're a ninny," to Dad's stupid report?

Not really.

Wait, what was this? Perfect Peter's homework essay!

Let's see what he's written, thought Henry. Perfect Peter's essay appeared on the screen, titled, "Why I love my teacher".

Poor Peter, thought Henry. What a boring title. Let's see if I can improve it for him.

Tap tap tap.

Peter's essay was now called, "Why I hate my teacher."

That's more like it, thought Henry. He read on.

"My teacher is the best. She's kind, she's fun, and she makes learning a joy. I am so lucky to be in Miss Lovely's class. Hip hip hooray for Miss Lovely."

Oh dear. Worse and worse, thought Horrid Henry. Tap tap tap.

"My teacher is the worst." Still missing something, thought Henry.

Tap tap.

"My fat teacher is the worst."

That's more like it, thought Henry. Now for the rest.

Tap tap tap tap tap.

"My fat teacher is the worst. She's mean, she's horrible, and she makes learning a misery. I am so unlucky to be in Miss Ugly's class. Boo hiss for Miss Ugly."

Much better.

Now that's what I call an essay, thought Horrid Henry. He pressed "Save", then switched off the computer and tiptoed back to bed.

"ARRRGGHHHH!"

"AAAHHHH!"

"NOOOOO!"

Horrid Henry jumped out of bed. Mum was shrieking. Dad was shrieking. Peter was shrieking.

Honestly, couldn't anyone get any rest around here? He stomped down the stairs.

Everyone was gathered round the computer.

"Do something!" shouted Dad. "I need that report now."

"I'm trying!" shouted Mum. She pressed a few keys.

"It's jammed," she said.

"My essay!" wailed Perfect Peter.

"My spreadsheet!" wailed Mum.

"My report!" wailed Dad.

"What's wrong?" said Henry.

"The computer's broken!" said Dad.

"How I hate these horrible machines," said Mum.

"You've got to fix it," said Dad. "I've got to hand in my report this morning."

"I can't," said Mum. "The computer won't let me in."

"I don't understand," said Dad. "We've never needed a password before."

Suddenly Horrid Henry realised what was wrong. He'd set a new password. No one could use the computer without it. Mum and Dad didn't know anything about passwords. All Horrid Henry had to do to fix the computer was to type in the password "Smelly Socks."

"I might be able to help, Dad," said Horrid Henry.

"Really?" said Dad. He looked doubtful.

"Are you sure?" said Mum. She looked doubtful.

"I'll try," said Horrid Henry. He sat down in front of the computer. "Whoops, no I can't," said Horrid Henry.

"Why not?" said Mum.

"I'm banned," said Henry. "Remember?"

"All right, you're unbanned," said Dad, scowling. "Just hurry up."

"I have to be at school with my essay in ten minutes!" moaned Peter.

"And I have to get to work!" moaned Mum.

"I'll do my best," said Horrid Henry slowly. "But this is a very hard problem to

39

solve."

He tapped a few keys and frowned at the screen.

"Do you know what's wrong, Henry?" asked Dad.

"The hard disk is disconnected from the harder disk, and the hardest disk has slipped," said Horrid Henry.

"Oh," said Dad.

"Ahh," said Mum.

"Huunh?" said Perfect Peter.

"You learn about that stuff in computer class next year," said Horrid Henry. "Now stand back, everyone, you're making me nervous."

Mum, Dad, and Peter stepped back.

"You're our last hope, Henry," said Mum.

"I will fix this on one condition, " said Henry.

"Anything," said Dad.

"Anything," said Mum.

"Deal," said Horrid Henry, and typed in the password.

Whirr! Whirr! Spit! Horrid Henry scooped up Mum's spreadsheet, Dad's report, and Perfect Peter's essay from the printer and handed them round.

"Thank you so much," said Dad.
"Thank you so much," said Mum.

Perfect Peter beamed at his beautifully printed essay, then put it carefully into his school bag. He'd never handed in a printed essay before. He couldn't wait to see what Miss Lovely said.

"Oh my goodness, Peter, what a smart looking essay you've written!" said Miss Lovely.

"It's all about you, Miss Lovely," said Peter, beaming. "Would you like to read it?"

"Of course," said Miss Lovely. "I'll read it to the class."

She cleared her throat and began:

"Why I ha—" Miss Lovely stopped reading. Her face went pink. "Peter!" she gasped. "Go straight to the head! Now!"

"But – but – is it because my essay is so good?" squeaked Peter.

"NO!" said Miss Lovely.

"Waaaaahhh!" wailed Perfect Peter.

PEEEEOWWWW! BANG! RAT-A-
TAT- TAT! Another intergalactic robot
bit the dust. Now, what shall I play next?
thought Horrid Henry happily. Snake
Masters Revenge lll? Zippy Zapper?
Best of all, Perfect Peter had been banned

from the computer for a week, after Miss Lovely had phoned Mum and Dad to tell them about Peter's rude essay. Peter blamed Henry. Henry blamed the computer.

3

....

HORRID HENRY
GOES TO WORK

"It's your turn!"

"No, it's yours!"

"Yours!"

"Yours!"

"I took Henry last year!" said Mum.

Dad paused. "Are you sure?"

"YES," said Mum.

"Are you sure you're sure?" said Dad.
He looked pale.

"Of course I'm sure!" said Mum.
"How could I forget?"

Tomorrow was take your child to

work day'. Mum wanted to take Peter. Dad wanted to take Peter. Unfortunately, someone had to take Henry.

Only today Dad's boss had said how much he was looking forward to meeting Dad's lovely son. "Of course I'll be bringing my boy, Bill," said Big Boss. "He's a great kid. Good as gold. Smart as a whip. Superb footballer. Brilliant at maths. Plays trumpet like a genius. Perfect manners. Yep, I sure am proud of Bill."

Dad tried not to hate Bill. He failed.

"Now listen, Henry," said Dad. "You're coming to work with me tomorrow. I'm warning you, my boss is bringing *his* son. From what I hear he's perfect."

"Like me?" said Peter. "I'd love to meet him. We could swap good deed ideas! Do you think he'd like to join my Best Boys Club?"

"You're going to Mum's work," said Dad sadly. "I'm taking Henry."

"Cool!" said Henry. A day out of school! A day at the office! "I want to play computer games. And eat doughnuts! And surf the web!"

"NO!" said Dad. "An office is a place where people work. I want perfect behaviour. My boss is very strict. Don't let me down, Henry."

"Of course I won't," said Horrid Henry. He was outraged. How could Dad think such a thing? The only trouble was, how could Henry have any fun with a boring goody-goody like Bill around?

"Remember what I said, Henry," said Dad the next morning, as they arrived at his office. "Be nice to Bill. Do what he says. He's the boss's son. Try to be as good as he is."

"All right," said Henry sourly.

Dad's boss came to welcome them.

"Ah, you must be Henry!" said Big Boss. "This is my son, Bill."

"So pleased to meet you, Henry," said Bossy Bill.

"Huh," grunted Horrid Henry.

He looked at Bossy Bill. He was wearing a jacket and tie. His face was gleaming. His shoes were so polished Henry could see his dirty face in them. Just his luck to get stuck all day with boring old Bossy Bill.

"Right, boys, your first job is to make tea for everyone in the meeting room," said Big Boss.

"Do I have to?" said Horrid Henry.

"Henry!" said Dad.

"Yes," said Big Boss. "That's six teas, one sugar in each."

"Gee thanks, Dad!" said Bossy Bill. "I love making tea."

"Whoopee," muttered Horrid Henry.

Big Boss beamed and left the room. Horrid Henry was alone with Bossy Bill.

The moment Big Boss left, Bill's face changed.

"Why doesn't he make his own stupid tea!" he snarled.

"I thought you loved making tea," said Horrid Henry. Maybe things were looking up.

"No way," said Bossy Bill. "What am I, a servant? You make it."

"You make it!" said Horrid Henry.

"You make it!" said Bossy Bill.

"No," said Henry.

"Yes," said Bill. "It's my dad's company and you have to do what I say."

"No I don't!" said Henry.

"Yes you do," said Bill.

"I don't work for you," said Henry.

"Yeah, but your dad works for *my* dad," said Bossy Bill. "If you don't do what I say I'll tell my dad to fire your dad."

Horrid Henry glared at Bossy Bill, then slowly switched on the kettle. When he was king he'd build a shark tank specially for Bill.

Bossy Bill folded his arms and smirked as Henry poured hot water over the teabags. What a creep, thought Henry, licking his fingers and dipping them into the sugar bowl.

"You're disgusting," said Bossy Bill. "I'm telling on you."

"Go ahead," said Henry, licking sugar off his fingers. Next to his cousin Stuck-up Steve, Bossy Bill was the yuckiest kid he had ever met.

"Hey, I've got a great idea," said Bill. "Let's put salt in the tea instead of sugar."

Horrid Henry hesitated. But hadn't Dad said to do what Bill told him?

"Okay," said Henry.

Bossy Bill poured a heaped teaspoon of salt into every cup.

"Now watch this," said Bill.

"Thank you, Bill," said Mr String. "Aren't you clever!"

"Thank you, Bill," said Ms Bean.

54

"Aren't you wonderful!"

"Thanks, Bill," said Big Boss. "How's the tea, everyone?"

"Delicious," said Mr String. He put down the cup.

"Delightful," said Ms Bean. She put down the cup.

"Umm," said Dad. He put down the cup.

Then Big Boss took a sip. His face curdled.

"Disgusting!" he gasped, spitting out the tea. "Bleeeach! Who put salt in this?"

"Henry did," said Bill.

Horrid Henry was outraged.

"Liar!" said Henry. "You did!"

"This tea is revolting," said Mr String.

"Horrible," said Ms Bean.

"I tried to stop him, Dad, but he just wouldn't listen," said Bossy Bill.

"I'm disappointed
in you, Henry," said
Big Boss. "Bill
would never do
anything like this."
He glanced at Dad.
Dad looked as if he
wished an alien

spaceship would beam him up.

"But I didn't do it!" said Henry. He
stared at Bill. What a creep!

"Now run along boys, and help answer
the phones. Bill will
show you how,
Henry," said Big
Boss.

Horrid Henry
followed Bill out of
the meeting room.
Beware, Bill, he
thought. I'll get you for this.

Bill sat down at a huge desk and swung his feet up.

"Now copy me," he said. "Answer the phones just like I do."

Ring ring.

"Hello, Elephant House!" said Bill.

Ring ring.

"Hello! Tootsie's Take-Away!" said Bill.

Ring ring.

"Hello! Pizza Parlour!" said Bill.

Ring ring.

"Go on, Henry, answer it."

"No!" said Henry. After what had just

happened with the tea, he'd never trust
Bill again.

Ring ring.

"What are you, chicken?" said Bill.

"No," said Henry.

"Then go on. *I* did it."

Ring ring ring ring.

"All right," said Henry. He picked up
the phone. He'd just do it once.

"Hello Smelly!
You're fired!"

Silence.

"Is that you,
Henry?" said Big
Boss on the other
end of the phone.

Eeek!

"Wrong number!" squeaked Horrid
Henry, and slammed down the phone.
Uh oh. Now he was in trouble. Big big
trouble.

Big Boss stormed
into the room.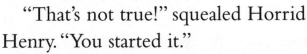

"What's going on in
here?"

"I tried to stop him,
but he just wouldn't
listen," said Bossy Bill.

"That's not true!" squealed Horrid
Henry. "You started it."

"As if," said Bossy Bill.

"And what have you been doing, son?"
asked Big Boss.

"Testing the phones for you," said
Bossy Bill. "I think there's a fault on line
2. I'll fix it in a minute."

"That's my little genius," beamed Big
Boss. He glared at Henry. Henry glared
back.

"I told you to follow Bill's example!"
hissed Dad.

"I did!" hissed Henry.

59

Bossy Bill and Big Boss exchanged pitying glances.

"He's not usually like this," lied Dad. He looked as if he wished a whirlwind would whisk him away.

"I am usually like this!" said Henry. "Just not today!"

"No pocket money for a year if there's any more trouble," muttered Dad.

This was so unfair. Why should he get blamed when it was absolutely definitely not his fault?

"I'll give you one more chance," said Big Boss. He handed Henry a stack of papers. "Photocopy these for the meeting this afternoon," he said. "If there are any more problems I will ask your father to take you home."

Take him home! Dad would never ever forgive him. He was mad enough at Henry already. And it was all Bill's fault.

60

Scowling, Horrid Henry followed Bill
into the photocopy room.

"Ha ha ha ha ha, I got you into
trouble!" chortled Bill.

Horrid Henry resisted the urge to
mash Bossy Bill into tiny bite-sized
chunks. Instead, Horrid Henry started to
think. Even if he was good as gold all day

it would mean Bill had won. He had to
come up with a plan to get back at Bill.
Fast. But what? Anything awful Bill did
Henry was sure to get the blame. No one
would believe Henry hadn't done it. If
his plan was to work, Bill had to be
caught red-handed.

And then Horrid Henry had it. A
perfectly brilliant, spectacularly evil plan.
A plan to end all plans. A plan to go
down in history. A plan – but there was
no time to lose congratulating himself.

Bossy Bill snatched the papers from
Henry's hand.

"I get to do the photocopying because
it's *my* dad's office," he said. "If you're
good I might let you hand out the
papers."

"Whatever you say," said Horrid
Henry humbly. "After all, you're the
boss."

"Too right I am," said Bossy Bill. "Everyone has to do what I say."

"Of course," said Horrid Henry agreeably. "Hey, I've got a great idea," he added after a moment, "why don't we make horrid faces, photocopy them and hang the pictures all round the meeting room?"

Bossy Bill's eyes gleamed. "Yeah!" he said. He stuck out his tongue. He made a monkey face. He twisted his lips. "Heh heh heh." Then he paused. "Wait a minute. We'd be recognised."

Aaargh! Horrid Henry hadn't thought of that. His beautiful plan crumpled

before him. Bill would win. Henry would
lose. The terrible image of Bossy Bill
laughing at him from here to eternity
loomed before him. NO! No one ever
tricked Horrid Henry and lived. I need a
change of plan, thought Henry
desperately. And then he knew what had
to be done. It was risky. It was dangerous.
But it was the only way.

"I know," said Horrid Henry. "Let's
photocopy our bottoms instead."

"Yeah!" said Bossy Bill. "I was just
going to suggest that."

"I get to go first," said Horrid Henry,
shoving Bill out of the way.

"No, I do!" said Bill, shoving him
back. YES! thought Horrid Henry, as Bill
hopped onto the photocopier. "*You* can
paste up the pictures in the meeting
room."

"Great!" said Henry. He could tell

what Bill was thinking. He'd get his dad to come in while Henry was sellotaping pictures of bottoms around the meeting room.

"I'll just get the sellotape," said Henry.

"You do that," said Bossy Bill, as the photocopier whirred into life.

Horrid Henry ran down the hall into Big Boss's office.

"Come quick, Bill's in trouble!" said Horrid Henry.

Big Boss dropped the phone and raced down the hall after Henry.

"Hold on, Bill, Daddy's coming!" he shrieked, and burst into the photocopy room.

There was Bossy Bill, perched on the photocopier, his back to the door, singing merrily:

"One bottom, two bottoms, three bottoms, four,

Five bottoms, six bottoms, seven bottoms, more!"

"Bill!" screamed Big Boss.

"It was Henry!" screamed Bossy Bill. "I was just testing the photocopier to make sure—"

"Be quiet, Bill!" shouted Big Boss. "I saw what you were doing."

"I tried to stop him but he just wouldn't listen," said Horrid Henry.

Horrid Henry spent a lovely rest of the day at Dad's office. After Bill was grounded for a month and sent home in disgrace, Henry twirled all the chairs round and round. He sneaked up behind people and shouted, "Boo!" Then he ate doughnuts, played computer games, and surfed the web. Boy, working in an office is fun, thought Horrid Henry. I'm going to enjoy getting a job when I grow up.

4

HORRiD HENRY
AND THE
DEMON DINNER LADY

"You're not having a packed lunch and that's final," yelled Dad.

"It's not fair!" yelled Horrid Henry. "Everyone in my class has a packed lunch."

"N–O spells no," said Dad. "It's too much work. And you never eat what I pack for you."

"But I hate school dinners!" screamed Henry. "I'm being poisoned!" He clutched his throat. "Dessert today was— bleeeach—fruit salad! And it had worms in it! I can feel them slithering in my stomach

– uggghh!" Horrid Henry fell to the floor, gasping and rasping.

Mum continued watching TV.

Dad continued watching TV.

"I love school dinners," said Perfect Peter. "They're so nutritious and delicious. Especially those lovely spinach salads."

"Shut up, Peter!" snarled Henry.

"Muuuum!" wailed Peter. "Henry told me to shut up!"

"Don't be horrid, Henry!" said Mum. "You're not having a packed lunch and that's that."

70

Horrid Henry and his parents had been fighting about packed lunches for weeks. Henry was desperate to have a packed lunch. Actually, he was desperate *not* to have a school dinner.

Horrid Henry hated school dinners. The stinky smell. The terrible way Sloppy Sally ladled the food *splat!* on his tray so that most of it splashed all over him. And the food! Queueing for hours for revolting ravioli and squashed tomatoes. The lumpy custard. The blobby mashed potatoes. Horrid Henry could not bear it any longer.

"Oh please," said Henry. "I'll make the packed lunch myself." Wouldn't that be great! He'd fill his lunchbox with four packs of crisps, chocolate, doughnuts, cake, lollies, and one grape. Now that's what I call a real lunch, thought Henry.

Mum sighed.

Dad sighed.

They looked at each other.

"If you promise that everything in your lunchbox will get eaten, then I'll do a packed lunch for you," said Dad.

"Oh thank you thank you thank you!" said Horrid Henry. "Everything will get eaten, I promise." Just not by me, he thought gleefully. Packed lunch room, here I come. Food fights, food swaps, food fun at last. Yippee!

Horrid Henry strolled into the packed lunch room. He was King Henry the

Horrible, surveying his unruly subjects.
All around him children were screaming
and shouting, pushing and shoving,
throwing food and trading treats. Heaven!
Horrid Henry smiled happily and opened
his Terminator Gladiator lunchbox.

Hmmn. An egg salad sandwich. On
brown bread. With crusts. Yuck! But he
could always swap it for one of Greedy
Graham's stack of chocolate spread
sandwiches. Or one of Rude Ralph's jam

rolls. That was the great thing about packed lunches, thought Henry. Someone always wanted what you had. No one *ever* wanted someone else's school dinner. Henry shuddered.

But those bad days were behind him, part of the dim and distant past. A horror story to tell his grandchildren. Henry could see it now. A row of horrified toddlers, screaming and crying while he told terrifying tales of stringy stew and soggy semolina.

Now, what else? Henry's fingers closed on something round. An apple. Great, thought Henry, he could use it for target practice, and the carrots would be perfect for poking Gorgeous Gurinder when she wasn't looking.

Henry dug deeper. What was buried right at the bottom? What was hidden under the celery sticks and the granola bar? Oh boy! Crisps! Henry loved crisps. So salty! So crunchy! So yummy! His mean, horrible parents only let him have crisps once a week. Crisps! What bliss! He could taste their delicious saltiness already. He wouldn't share them with anyone, no matter how hard they begged. Henry tore open the bag and reached in—

Suddenly a huge shadow fell over him. A fat greasy hand shot out. Snatch! Crunch. Crunch.

Horrid Henry's crisps were gone.

Henry was so shocked that for a moment he could not speak. "Wha— wha—what was that?" gasped Henry as a gigantic woman waddled between the tables. "She just stole my crisps!"

"That," said Rude Ralph grimly, "was Greta. She's the demon dinner lady."

"Watch out for her!" squealed Sour Susan.

"She's the sneakiest snatcher in school," wailed Weepy William.

What? A dinner lady who snatched food instead of dumping it on your plate? How could this be? Henry stared as Greasy Greta patrolled up and down the aisles. Her piggy eyes darted from side to side. She ignored Aerobic Al's carrots. She ignored Tidy Ted's yoghurt. She ignored Goody-Goody Gordon's orange.

Then suddenly—

Snatch! Chomp. Chomp.
Sour Susan's sweets were gone.
Snatch! Chomp. Chomp.
Dizzy Dave's doughnut was
gone.

Snatch! Chomp.
Chomp. Beefy Bert's
biscuits were gone.
Moody Margaret
looked up from her
lunch.

"Don't look up!" shrieked Susan. Too
late! Greasy Greta swept Margaret's food
away, stuffing Margaret's uneaten
chocolate bar into her fat wobbly cheeks.

"Hey, I wasn't finished!" screamed
Margaret. Greasy Greta ignored her and
marched on. Weepy William tried to hide
his toffees under his cheese sandwich. But
Greasy Greta wasn't fooled.

Snatch! Gobble. Gobble. The toffees

77

vanished down Greta's gaping gob.

"Waaah," wailed William. "I want my toffees!"

"No sweets in school," barked Greasy Greta. She marched up and down, up and down, snatching and grabbing, looting and devouring, wobbling and gobbling.

Why had no one told him there was a demon dinner lady in charge of the packed lunch room?

"Why didn't you warn me about her, Ralph?" demanded Henry.

Rude Ralph shrugged. "It wouldn't have done any good. She is unstoppable."

We'll see about that, thought Henry. He glared at Greta. No way would Greasy Greta grab his food again.

On Tuesday Greta snatched Henry's doughnut.

On Wednesday Greta snatched Henry's cake.

On Thursday Greta snatched Henry's biscuits.

On Friday, as usual, Horrid Henry persuaded Anxious Andrew to swap his crisps for Henry's granola bar. He persuaded Kung-Fu Kate to swap her chocolates for Henry's raisins. He persuaded Beefy Bert to swap his biscuits for Henry's carrots. But what was the use of being a brilliant food trader, thought Henry miserably, if Greasy Greta just swooped and snaffled his hard-won treats?

Henry tried hiding his desserts. He tried eating his desserts secretly. He tried tugging them back. But it was no use.

The moment he snapped open his lunch box – SNATCH! Greasy Greta grabbed the goodies.

Something had to be done.

"Mum," complained Henry, "there's a demon dinner lady at school snatching our sweets."

"That's nice, Henry," said Mum, reading her newspaper.

"Dad," complained Henry, "there's a demon dinner lady at school snatching our sweets."

"Good," said Dad. "You eat too many sweets."

"We're not allowed to bring sweets to school, Henry," said Perfect Peter.

"But it's not fair!" squealed Henry. "She takes crisps, too."

"If you don't like it, go back to school dinners," said Dad.

"No!" howled Henry. "I hate school dinners!" Watery gravy with bits. Lumpy surprise with lumps. Gristly glop with

globules. Food with its own life slopping about on his tray. NO! Horrid Henry couldn't face it. He'd fought so hard for a packed lunch. Even a packed lunch like the one Dad made, fortified with eight essential minerals and vitamins, was better than going back to school dinners.

He could, of course, just eat healthy foods. Greta never snatched those. Henry imagined his lunchbox, groaning with alfalfa sprouts on wholemeal brown bread studded with chewy bits. Ugh! Bleeeach! Torture!

He had to keep his packed lunch. But he had to stop Greta. He just had to.

And then suddenly Henry had a brilliant, spectacular idea. It was so brilliant that for a moment he could hardly believe he'd thought of it. Oh boy, Greta, thought Henry gleefully, are you going to be sorry you messed with me.

Lunchtime. Horrid Henry sat with his lunchbox unopened. Rude Ralph was armed and ready beside him. Now, where was Greta?

Thump. Thump. Thump. The floor shook as the demon dinner lady started her food patrol. Horrid Henry waited

until she was almost behind him. SNAP!
He opened his lunchbox.

SNATCH! The familiar greasy hand
shot out, grabbed Henry's biscuits and
shovelled them into her mouth. Her
terrible teeth began to chomp.

And then—-

"Yiaowwww! Aaaarrrgh!" A terrible
scream echoed through the packed lunch
room.

Greasy Greta turned purple. Then pink. Then bright red.

"Yiaowwww!" she howled. "I need to cool down! Gimme that!" she screeched, snatching Rude Ralph's doughnut and stuffing it in her mouth.

"Aaaarrrgh!" she choked. "I'm on fire! Water! Water!"

She grabbed a pitcher of water, poured it on top of herself, then ran howling down the aisle and out the door.

For a moment there was silence. Then the entire packed lunch room started clapping and cheering.

"Wow, Henry," said Greedy Graham, "what did you do to her?"

"Nothing," said Horrid Henry. "She just tried my special recipe. Hot chilli powder biscuits, anyone?"

**The HORRID HENRY books
by Francesca Simon**

Illustrated by Tony Ross

Each book contains four stories

HORRID HENRY

Henry is dragged to dancing class against his will; vies with Moody Margaret to make the yuckiest Glop, goes camping in France and tries to be good like Perfect Peter – but not for long.

HORRID HENRY
AND THE SECRET CLUB

Horrid Henry gets an injection, torments
his little brother Perfect Peter, creates
havoc at his own birthday party, and plans
sweet revenge when Moody Margaret
won't let him into her Secret Club.

HORRID HENRY
TRICKS THE TOOTH FAIRY

(Originally published as
Horrid Henry and the Tooth Fairy)

Horrid Henry tries to trick the Tooth
Fairy into giving him more money, sends
Moody Margaret packing, causes his
teachers to run screaming from school,
and single-handedly wrecks a wedding.

HORRID HENRY'S NITS

Scratch. Scratch. Scratch. Horrid Henry has nits – and he's on a mission to give them to everyone else too. After that, he can turn his attention to wrecking the school trip, ruining his parents' dinner party, and terrifying Perfect Peter.

HORRID HENRY'S
HAUNTED HOUSE

Horrid Henry slugs it out with Perfect Peter over the remote control, stays in a haunted house and gets a nasty shock, discovers where X marks the spot in the hidden treasure competition and stars on TV.

HORRID HENRY
GETS RICH QUICK

(Originally published as
Horrid Henry Strikes It Rich)

Horrid Henry tries to sell off Perfect
Peter and get rich, makes sure he gets
the presents he wants for Christmas,
sabotages Sports Day at school – and
runs away from home.

HORRID HENRY AND THE MUMMY'S CURSE

Horrid Henry indulges his favourite hobby – collecting Gizmos – has a bad time with his spelling homework, puts about a rumour that there's a shark in the swimming pool, and spooks Perfect Peter with the mummy's curse.

HORRID HENRY
AND THE
BOGEY BABYSITTER

Horrid Henry encounters the babysitter
from hell, traumatizes his parents on a car
journey, goes trick or treating at
Hallowe'en, and invades Moody
Margaret's Secret Club.

And for younger children

DON'T BE HORRID, HENRY

Illustrated by Kevin McAleenan
A full-colour picture book introducing
Horrid Henry to younger readers.

A HANDFUL OF HORRID HENRY

Three hilarious books
in one volume:

Horrid Henry
Horrid Henry and the Secret Club
Horrid Henry Tricks the Tooth Fairy

A HELPING OF HORRID HENRY

More hilarious stories, in one
bumper volume:

Horrid Henry's Nits
Horrid Henry Gets Rich Quick
Horrid Henry's Haunted House